My Dad

OTHER BOOKS BY NIKI DALY

Not So Fast, Songololo

Papa Lucky's Shadow

Copyright © 1995 by Niki Daly
All rights reserved including the right of reproduction in whole or in part in any form.
Margaret K. McElderry Books
An imprint of Simon & Schuster Children's Publishing Division
1230 Avenue of the Americas
New York, New York 10020
First edition
Printed on recycled paper
Designed by Nancy Williams
The text of this book is set in Plantin Light.
The illustrations are rendered in watercolor and pencil.
10 9 8 7 6 5 4 3 2 1

Library of Congress Cataloging-in-Publication Data
Daly, Niki.
My dad : story and pictures / by Niki Daly. — 1st ed.
p.   cm.
Summary: A father's drinking causes pain and embarrassment to his family, until he begins to attend
Alcoholics Anonymous meetings.
ISBN 0-689-50620-1
[1. Alcoholism—Fiction.   2. Fathers—Fiction.]   I. Title.
PZ7.D1715My   1995
[E]—dc20   94-14455

My Dad

story and pictures by Niki Daly

MARGARET K. McELDERRY BOOKS

My daddy, he plays rock 'n' roll
He goes doo wah, doo wah, oh bless my soul.

It was Friday evening and Dad was in a sparky mood. Empty beer bottles and Dad's pals fought for space around the table. When I looked in, Dad gave me a funny, boozy smile.

I like Dad when he is jolly, but I don't like him when he is boozy and silly. But that's how he always ends up on Friday nights when all the singing and joking stop and his pals pile out the front door.

My dad says I have a good ear for music. I've learned a few strumming chords from him that I can turn into songs on the guitar he made for me.

My dad is very good with his hands. He can saw through lumber as easily as cutting off a chunk of bread. I often watch him work as he turns out all kinds of things, like the fancy stand he made for Mom's special ornaments. The smell of wood glue, sawdust, and Dad fills the little backyard shed on warm summer days.

The only problem with Dad's woodwork is this: If anyone says *anything* nice about it, Dad insists on giving the piece to that person. Mom has to bite her tongue as things are carried out of the house— especially on Friday nights.

Lying in the dark on Friday nights, Gracie and I often hear Mom and Dad arguing.

Gracie and I love putting on a show. She dances and I play my guitar and sing. Dad is very proud of us. He says that Gracie is the "apple of his eye," and that I am his "sunnyboy." He says he'd be lost without us.

"How much do you love us?" Gracie once asked.

"More than all the tea in China," Dad answered.

"More than all the booze in a bottle?" I asked. I meant it as a joke, but Dad looked sad, and angry.

Later I found him in his shed. He was hammering a nail into a piece of wood, as though it needed punishing.

"Dad," I said nervously, "I'm sorry about what I said." Dad stopped banging, and then a terrible thing happened. He started to cry. It was horrible. I didn't know that a dad could cry like that. It was like the sky breaking open. There were so many tears it scared me.

"I won't tell, Dad. I won't tell," was all I could say.

Mr. Dickie, our music teacher, has asked Gracie and me to do something at a Friday-night school concert. We rehearse at home every day after school, but as soon as we hear Dad's hand touch the front door, we stop. We don't want our school to see what Dad is like on Friday nights, so we don't want Dad to know about our concert.

And Dad's drinking seems to be getting worse. He and Mom argue almost every night.

One night, Gracie and I woke up to loud voices in the kitchen. We got up and slowly walked down the dark hall. In the glare of the kitchen light we saw Mom and Dad fighting over a bottle. Mom was trying to empty the bottle into the sink while Dad kept shouting, "I'm not an alcoholic! I'm not an alcoholic!"

When we were back in bed Mom tucked us in.

"What's an alcoholic, Mom?" I asked.

"It's someone who should never drink alcohol, because it harms them and their family," she answered.

"Is Dad like that?" asked Gracie in a frightened voice.

"I think he is," said Mom. "But I don't want you to worry about it."

But I *was* worried. I had a dad who was an alcoholic.

On the night of the concert we left for school before Dad got home.
Backstage, Mom wished us luck.

It was great being on the stage. I could feel we were doing okay.
But as Gracie was dancing across the stage to my last verse, a loud
voice shook up the hall.

"THAT'S MY BOY!"

It was Dad! Somehow, he'd found out about us.

"Show them, kids! You show them!" His voice thrashed recklessly
around the hall.

My fingers went limp and lost their grip on the neck of my guitar. The music withered as the words of the song seemed to sink into my stomach. Gracie's footsteps faltered, and then she froze. Tears glimmered in the corners of her eyes as she stood with her toes pointing nowhere. I took her hand and led her off the stage. The only words left in my head were, "I hate him!"

Dad was driven home by Mr. Dickie while Mom, Gracie, and I walked. Mom kept saying, "We need help, we really need help." Gracie and I didn't talk. But I could feel our thoughts, and they were cold and lonely.

Since then, when we're at home, Gracie and I just hang around feeling down. I pick up my guitar and start to play.

My daddy's like a guitar that's lost its shine
All out of tune and out of time.

Maybe it was our hate for Dad's drinking, maybe it was our love for Dad, or perhaps it was something Mr. Dickie said to Dad as they drove home that night after the school concert. But something good happened soon afterward. Instead of drinking with his buddies, Dad started going with Mr. Dickie to a place where alcoholics meet and help each other. Mom told us that Mr. Dickie once had a drinking problem that led him to the AA meetings. She explained that AA stands for Alcoholics Anonymous.

Now it looks as though Dad is planning to join AA. Mom says that it's going to take a long time for Dad to beat the booze, and, in the meantime, he's going to need all our love and support.

Dad says he is sorry he has brought so much darkness into our home. Now that he knows he is sick, and an alcoholic, he wants to get better—like Mr. Dickie. Mom puts her arm around his shoulder.

"It's like finding out what the most important things in my life are," Dad says.

And then he reaches out to us.

In memory of my dad